Dear Parents:

Congratulations! Your child is taking the first steps on an exciting journey. The destination? Independent reading!

STEP INTO READING® will help your child get there. The program offers five steps to reading success. Each step includes fun stories and colorful art or photographs. In addition to original fiction and books with favorite characters, there are Step into Reading Non-Fiction Readers, Phonics Readers and Boxed Sets, Sticker Readers, and Comic Readers—a complete literacy program with something to interest every child.

Learning to Read, Step by Step!

Ready to Read   Preschool–Kindergarten
• big type and easy words • rhyme and rhythm • picture clues
For children who know the alphabet and are eager to begin reading.

Reading with Help   Preschool–Grade 1
• basic vocabulary • short sentences • simple stories
For children who recognize familiar words and sound out new words with help.

Reading on Your Own   Grades 1–3
• engaging characters • easy-to-follow plots • popular topics
For children who are ready to read on their own.

Reading Paragraphs   Grades 2–3
• challenging vocabulary • short paragraphs • exciting stories
For newly independent readers who read simple sentences with confidence.

Ready for Chapters   Grades 2–4
• chapters • longer paragraphs • full-color art
For children who want to take the plunge into chapter books but still like colorful pictures.

STEP INTO READING® is designed to give every child a successful reading experience. The grade levels are only guides; children will progress through the steps at their own speed, developing confidence in their reading.

Remember, a lifetime love of reading starts with a single step!

EwL

Special thanks to Diane Reichenberger, Cindy Ledermann, Sarah Lazar, Charnita Belcher, Tanya Mann, Julia Phelps, Nicole Corse, Sharon Woloszyk, Rita Lichtwardt, Carla Alford, Renee Reeser Zelnick, Rob Hudnut, David Wiebe, Shelley Dvi-Vardhana, Gabrielle Miles, Rainmaker Entertainment, and Walter P. Martishius

Published in the United States by Random House Children's Books, a division of Random House LLC, 1745 Broadway, New York, NY 10019, and in Canada by Random House of Canada Limited, Toronto, Penguin Random House Companies.

Step into Reading, Random House, and the Random House colophon are registered trademarks of Random House LLC.

Visit us on the Web!
StepIntoReading.com
randomhouse.com/kids

Educators and librarians, for a variety of teaching tools, visit us at RHTeachersLibrarians.com

ISBN 978-0-385-38296-0 (trade) — ISBN 978-0-375-97341-3 (lib. bdg.) —
ISBN 978-0-375-98242-2 (ebook)

Printed in the United States of America

10 9 8 7 6 5 4 3 2 1

Barbie
AND THE
SECRET DOOR

MAGIC FRIENDS

Adapted by Chelsea West

Based on the screenplay by Brian Hohlfeld

Illustrated by Ulkutay Design Group

Random House 🏠 New York

Princess Alexa is shy.

She just wants

to read her book.

Her mother wants her

to dance

at a big party.

Alexa tries to dance.

She trips!

Her friends gasp.

They stop dancing.

Alexa is embarrassed.

Alexa takes her book
to the garden.
She finds
a secret door.

The door sparkles.
Alexa opens the door
and goes inside.

Alexa enters
a magical world.
She is amazed!

She sees strange plants
and floating islands.
Two girls spot her.

Alexa meets
the two girls.
Their names are
Romy and Nori.

Alexa's hair stick turns
into a wand.
Alexa learns she
has magic powers!

Sniffers roll in!

They hunt magic.

The girls must hide.

Long ropes lift them

high into a tree.

Three unicorns
greet Alexa.
They are hiding
in a secret valley.

A bad princess
named Malucia wants
to steal all the magic
in the kingdom.

Malucia steals
Nola the fairy's magic.
She says that
the Queen Unicorn
will be next.

Nola warns Alexa
and her friends.
They must save
the Queen Unicorn
from Malucia.

Alexa turns a lily pad
into a flying carpet.
The friends fly away
to save
the Queen Unicorn.

They find
the Queen Unicorn!
But Malucia and her
helpers followed them.

Alexa's wand breaks!
Malucia's helpers
throw a net
over the unicorn.

Alexa fixes her wand.
It is not too late.
Malucia is back
in her castle.

Alexa runs
into the castle.
She tries to stop
Malucia with magic.

Malucia's helpers
grab Alexa.
Malucia laughs.

Her wand steals
Alexa's magic.
The wand
starts to crack!

Malucia's wand
shatters!
Alexa's magic is
too powerful for her.

All of the stolen
magic is returned.
Alexa's dress changes
into a beautiful gown.

The unicorns
thank Alexa
for saving them.

Alexa waves good-bye
to her new friends.

Alexa returns home.
She dances
in her new gown
at the big party!